THE VERY FIRST
LUCY GOOSE
BOOK

STEPHEN WEATHERILL

PRENTICE - HALL BOOKS FOR YOUNG READERS
A Division of Simon & Schuster, Inc.
New York

To Luke

Published by Prentice-Hall Books for Young Readers,
a division of Simon & Schuster, Inc.,
Simon & Schuster Building, 1230 Avenue of the Americas,
New York, NY 10020
Prentice-Hall Books for Young Readers is a trademark of
Simon & Schuster, Inc.

Printed in Belgium

10   9   8   7   6   5   4   3   2   1

ISBN 013-941910-X

LUCY GOOSE & THE FROGS

Lucy let the frog stay.

"Big softy."

...and two weeks later after a visit from the Midwife Toad.

"Mother and two thousand tadpoles all doing well."

Lucy had to make other bathing arrangements.

MAY

JUNE

JULY

The tadpoles spent the summer growing into little frogs.

Then the big day arrived to hop it.

"Bye Aunt Lucy"

A good long soak at last ..and now for our serial - Pond Life ♪♪

But three weeks later, on a cold and windy October night, Lucy heard a faint knock on the door.

KNOCK KNOCK

EAU de CABBP

..and...

We used to spend the winter sleeping in the reed beds..

..but they've been filled in.

Don't tell me. You used to sleep at the bottom of the lake...

...and it's been filled in too.

"You'd better come in," groaned Lucy.

6

Christmas Eve.

I'm dreaming of a Green Christmas

Look Aunt Lucy! Froggy Goes To Hollywood Christmas Special!

BANG

That night Lucy left a message for Santa.

Phew! Having two thousand young frogs as guests can be very tiring.

SANTA CLAUS

Outside, Santa was on his way.

Okay. Have you ever seen a flying reindeer?

Santa reads the message.

H'mm interesting. BMXs and computers get so boring.

Dear Santa
I'd like a nice BIG frog pond for my little green friends
Thanks. Lucy.

Fen End Dec. 24

On Christmas morning, Lucy woke to find a large present.

From Santa

7

A letter from Santa.

Santa's Castle, North Pole. Dec. 25

Dear Lucy, Please find enclosed 2001 tickets for the Froglands Nature Reserve.

Merry Christmas

S.C.

MAP
YOU ARE HERE

FROGLANDS
NATURE RESERVE
ADMIT THE BEARER

AFFIX PHOTO HERE

So as soon as all the little frogs were awake, they set off.

FROGLANDS
NATURE
VACANCY
RESERVE

The frogs were delighted and sang Lucy a goodbye song.

Happy New Year!

POND
FOR USE OF RESIDENTS ONLY.

♪ We love Lucy, ♪ She's our ♪ Goosey! ♪

LUCY GOOSE & THE BIRDBATH

A nosy horse came along and suggested blowing on the bath to melt the ice.

But it was so cold, the hair on his nose froze.

NEIGH MORE!

So far, they'd only managed to wake up a hedgehog.

VERY HELPFUL.

Why don't you leave it till spring and it'll melt by itself zzzzz

Some birds flew across to see what was happening.

Our water's frozen too.

What about the Black Pecker Bird? We can't leave him.

We'll have to take him with us.

We must go somewhere warmer. Other birds do. We must fly SOUTH!

BIRD BRAIN

ICE

So the birds flew south, taking the bath with them.

Always knew this hammock would come in handy one day.

TWEET!

TWEET TWEET!

HONK! HONK!

TWITTER

QUACK!

11

Meanwhile, thousands of miles south, El Ganso, the desert goose, had a problem.

It's no good, my little friend. All the water has dried up.

Getting any rain now is as likely as a tub full of iced water dropping on our heads.

Then they saw a dark shape in the sky.

A cloud?

Very noisy for a cloud. Must be a mirage.

No, it was the birds with Lucy's bath.

P.P.Phew.

Excuse me. Are we all right for Torremolinos?

Hey! Amigos! Down here!

In no time, Lucy's bath became a major tourist attraction.

COOL SPRINGS OASIS

TICKETS

Know where we can get any more ice?

LUCY'S SECRET ADMIRER

February 14th. St. Valentines Day.

Oh goody! Lots of cards from all my secret admirers.

But there were no cards for Lucy.

WATER RATES
L. Goose.
Fen End.
FINAL NOTICE

Duck Dick had a Valentine.

I'm so Lucky
You're my Ducky ×××

Noel Vole had a Valentine.

THE HOLE

NOEL VOLE IS MY LONE LOVE ××× ××××

Even the Toad, who wasn't quite awake yet.

ODE TO A TOAD
OF THE TOAD LITTLE IS KNOWED BUT A LOT IS OWED. ××××

"Nobody loves a goose", thought Lucy.

Meanwhile, in a nearby orchard, Godfrey the Gander was busy painting.

ROOSES ARE RED

Shut it, smarty! This is poetry.

Only one O in ROOSES Boss.

SWAN DISGUISE KIT
LOOK LIKE A SWAN

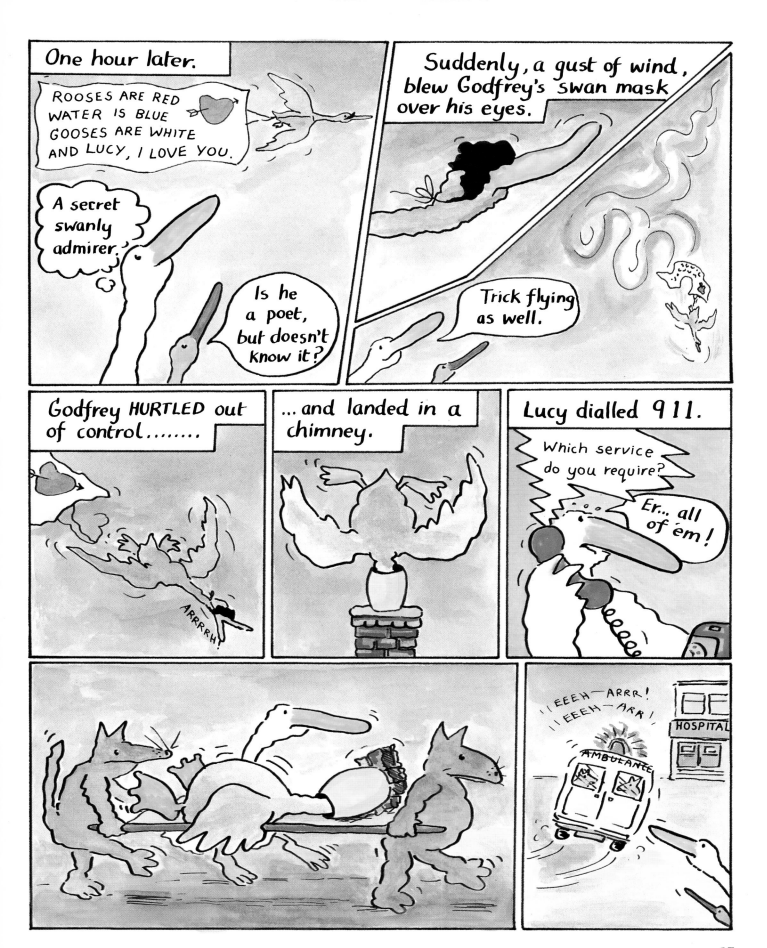

WAITING ROOM

OPERATING THEATER

Lucy waited while the brain surgeon operated to remove the chimney pot.

I wonder who my secret admirer is?

Chisel, nurse! The BIG hammer.

Godfrey!

Later that day.

These flowers are delicious, Godfrey.

To my secret admirer — Godfrey

Get well soon! Lucy X

16

THE DINNER PARTY

She looks in the cupboard

They were soon home with the groceries.

SUPERMARKET

Oh NO! I forgot Griselda doesn't eat tinned food. I'd better get it all out now.

CAULIFLOWER EARS

EXTRA MUSHY PEAS

Lucy and Dick tipped all the food into the bath.

We haven't time to cook it. Just mix it up well.

Finish the mixing Dick. I have to go and collect Griselda and Graham.

You might have to whisk it. Back soon!

?

The only animal I know with 'whiskers' is Noel Vole.

THE HOLE

Dick tried stirring the soup with Noel. It didn't seem to work.

Argh! Stop it! Glug...

19

HOW THE GOOSE LEARNED TO FLY

Betty Bantam had a very bad cold.

It's good of you to look after the nursery, Lucy.

No problem Betty.

Hi Kids!

BETTY BANTAM NURSERY

Looking after the nursery wasn't as easy as she thought.

Tell us a story Lucy.

How high can you fly?

You've got BIG feet.

TWEET TWEET!

EEEEEEEEK

EEE AH! EEE AW!

HELP! I'm stuck!

Alright! If you promise to be quiet, I'll tell you a story.

Tell us how the goose learned to fly.

SIZE 12.

Once upon a time, geese could not fly.

My Dad still can't fly.

24

...and that's how the goose learned to fly.

Just then the mailman arrived.

Two Get-Well cards for Miss Bantam.

The young birds made straight for his ankle.

Gerr off!

Stoppit!

"It's the way I tell 'em." said Lucy, as she watched the chase disappear over the fields.

THE END